For Hannah, Sam, and Ben

Published in the United States by Schwartz & Wade Books, an imprint of Random House
Children's Books, a division of Random House, Inc., New York.

Schwartz & Wade Books and colophon are trademarks of Random House, Inc.

www.randomhouse.com/kids

Educators and librarians, for a variety of teaching tools,
visit us at www.randomhouse.com/teachers

The text of this book is set in Opti Powell Old Style.
The illustrations are rendered in gouache.
Design by Annie Kelley

Library of Congress Cataloging-in-Publication Data
Russo, Marisabina.
The bunnies are not in their beds / by Marisabina Russo. —1st ed.
p. cm.
Summary: Some young rabbits would rather play than sleep,
much to their parents' chagrin.
ISBN 978-0-375-83961-0 (trade) — ISBN 978-0-375-93961-7 (lib. bdg.)
[1. Rabbits—Fiction. 2. Bedtime—Fiction.] I. Title.
PZ7.R9192 Bun 2007
[E]—dc22
2006002496

PRINTED IN CHINA
10 9 8 7 6 5 4 3 2 1
First Edition

Marisabina Russo

the bunnies are not in their beds

schwartz & wade books · new york

Nighttime is here.

Little bunnies are tucked in bed.

Good night, good night, sleep tight.

Mama sits in her chair and
Daddy sits in his.
All is quiet.

But then . . .

CLiCK CLAcK, CLiCK CLAcK.

What is that noise?
Sounds like the bunnies
are not in their beds.

Mama and Daddy tiptoe up the stairs,

open the door,

and what do they see?

Back to bed, little bunnies.

No more tracks on the floor.
See you in the morning.

Good night,
good night,
sleep tight.

All is quiet again.

Mama writes a birthday card to Grandma,

and Daddy reads a book.

But then...

CHUGGA-CHUGGA-CHUGGA.

What is that noise?
Sounds like the bunnies
are not in their beds.

Mama and Daddy
tiptoe up the stairs,
open the door,
and what do they see?

What are you doing, little bunnies?

No more tracks, no more trains.

No more mischief tonight.

Good night,

good night,

sleep tight.

All is quiet again.

Mama makes tea in her teapot

and Daddy sets out the cups.

But then . . .

CLIP CLOP, CLIP CLOP.

What is that noise?
Sounds like the bunnies
are not in their beds.

Mama and Daddy
tiptoe up the stairs,
open the door,
and what do they see?

What's going on, little bunnies?

You're not listening to us.

No more tracks, no more trains, no more horses.

No more mischief tonight.

Good night,

good night,

sleep tight.

All is quiet again.

Mama is sipping her tea

and Daddy is slicing some cake.

But then ...

ZOOM, ZOOM, VROOM!

What's all that noise?
Sounds like the bunnies
are not in their beds.

Mama and Daddy
walk up the stairs,
open the door,
and what do they see?

Little bunnies!

Back to bed before we

count to three.

No more tracks, no more trains,

no more horses, no more cars.

No more mischief.

One ... two ... three.

Good night,

good night,

sleep tight.

All is quiet again.

Mama turns off the lights

and Daddy pulls down the shades.

But then . . .

BOOM, BOOM, BOOM!
HONK, SQUONK, HONK!
CLASH, CLASH, SMASH!

What's all that noise?
Sounds like the bunnies
are not in their beds.

Mama and Daddy
march up the stairs,
open the door,
and what do they see?

There will be NO MORE NOISE, little bunnies!

Not the CLICK or the CLACK of a track.

Not the CHUGGA-CHUG-CHUG of a train.

Not the CLIP or the CLOP of a horse.

Not the ZOOM ZOOM or VROOM of a car.

Not the BOOM or the HONK or the CLASH

or the SMASH of a big bunny band.

Not a WIGGLE, not a GIGGLE,

NOT A SOUND.

Good night, good night, GOOD NIGHT!

Out go the lights.

All is quiet again.

Not a sound in the house.

The good little bunnies must be in their beds.

But then . . .

Tip
    tap.

Tippity
    tap.

What is that noise?
Sounds like the bunnies are *not*
  in their beds.

They tiptoe down the hall,
  open the door,
and what do they see?

Mama and Daddy
tucked into bed.
Fast asleep.
At last!

"Hooray!"
whisper the bunnies.

"We can play all night long!"

But then . . .

Yawn. Snuffle. Zzz, zzz, zzz.

What is that noise?

Sounds like the bunnies are all fast asleep.

Good night, every bunny, big and small.

Sweet bunny dreams to one and all.

Good night, good night, sleep tight.